Marjorie
Rose
Hakala

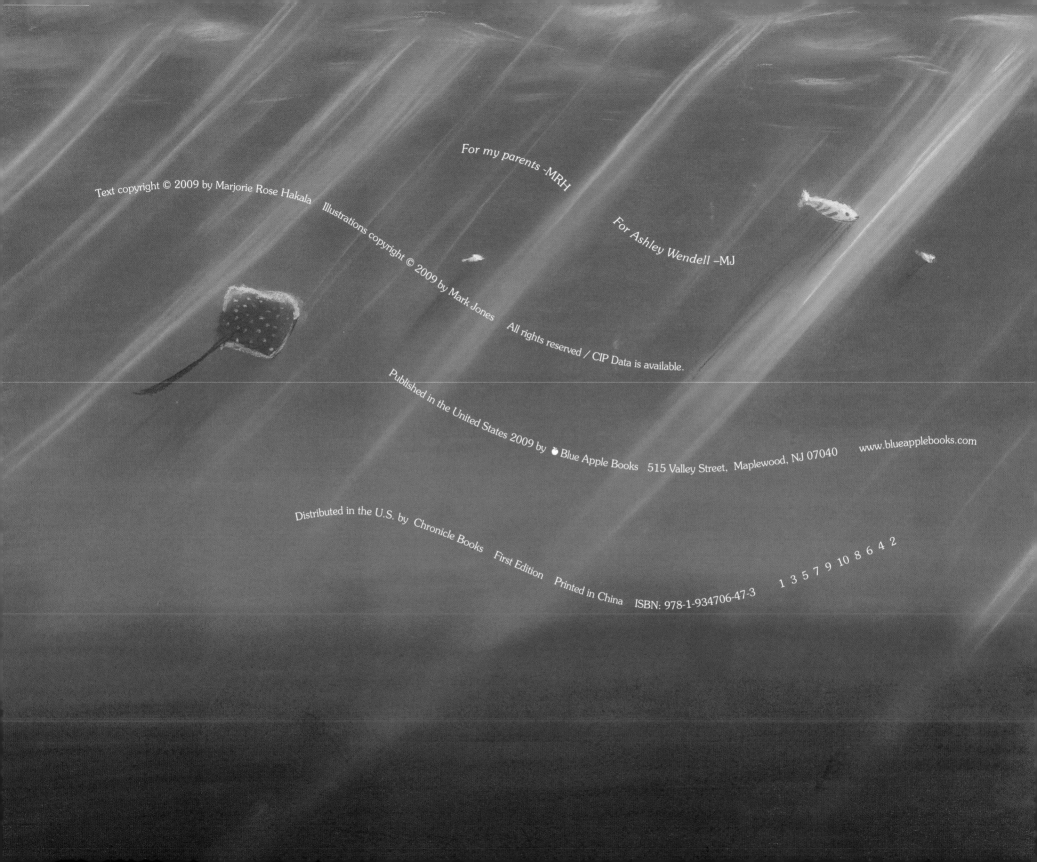

Published in the United States 2009 by 🍎 Blue Apple Books   515 Valley Street, Maplewood, NJ 07040   www.blueapplebooks.com

Distributed in the U.S. by Chronicle Books   First Edition   Printed in China   ISBN: 978-1-934706-47-3   1 3 5 7 9 10 8 6 4 2

Mermaid Dance

Marjorie Rose Hakala

illustrated by Mark Jones

BLUE APPLE BOOKS

The sun was setting on the ocean.

Waves lapped in and out,
    in and out,
      over the smooth sand
         and rough rocks.

The sky turned pink, then purple.

And when it turned a deep orange,

a mermaid came swimming

toward the beach.

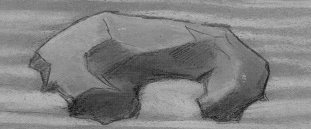

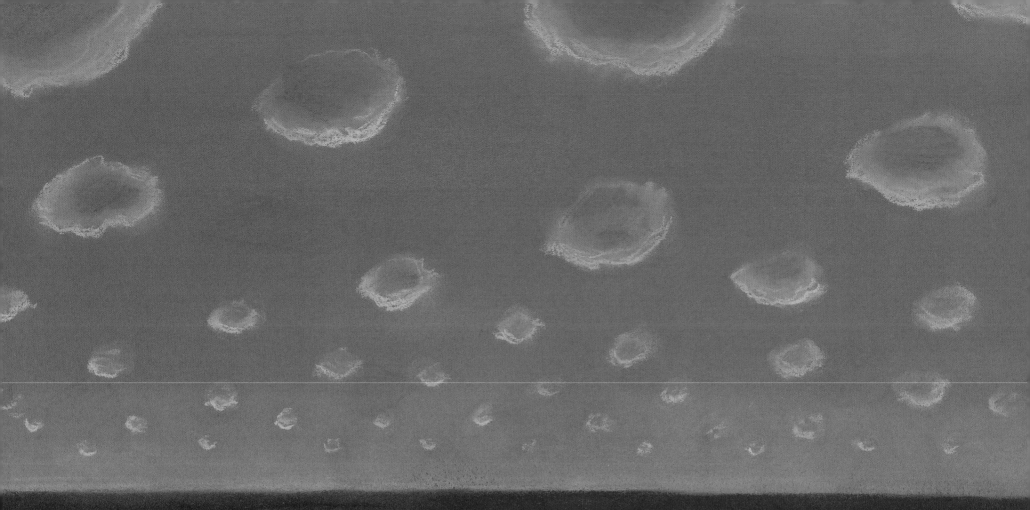

She pulled herself onto a rock in a little cove.

"Perfect," she said. "A perfect place to celebrate."

Then she waited for the moon to rise, and for the

high tide that would bring the cool, deep ocean.

As the waves washed higher,
a silver mermaid arrived,
then a green one,
then a gold.

They carried baskets
filled with food,
seashells and starfish.

A pink mermaid with corals in her hair

spread out a seaweed carpet.

"Come sit with me!" she called.

Other mermaids swam around
the cove draping strings of pearls,
seashells, and coral beads
from the low-hanging branches.

"I made these beads,"
boasted the youngest mermaid,
as she took them out of her basket.

"You made some of them,"
her sister said.
"And I made some. Some of them are very old."

Stars lit the sky. A few of the mermaids
lit driftwood fires and started preparing a feast.

The youngest mermaid pointed up.

"Look at the moon! Is it high enough now?

Is it time for the solstice party?"

"It's almost time," said the green mermaid.

"Come and help keep the birds away from our food."

The turtles and seagulls were curious.

Fish swam back and forth,

watching, wondering, waiting.

When the meal was ready,
everyone gathered to eat.

They ate as the tide rose,
until the waves washed
over the rocks and carried away
the seaweed mats.

The two sisters swam to the edge of the beach to where trees grew
and wild things lived, to where the water only came at the high full-moon tide.
The youngest had never been so close to a forest before.

"Do you see anything?"
she whispered.
"Hardly anything.
It's dark under the trees."

Two of the mermaids started to play
a song on a shell flute and drum.
The rest kicked into the water,
holding hands to dance.

"Let's dance for the first night of summer,"
said the blue mermaid.

The music grew stronger.

The deer and birds
and squirrels made their way
timidly out of the forest
to join the mermaids, the seagulls,
and the wild creatures of the ocean.

"Have you come to watch us?"

asked the youngest mermaid.

Some mermaids
whirled in a circle,
   others dove deep
in the water
and came rushing
   back to the surface.

The fish and turtles
   flitted in and out
of the dance.

All through the night,
they twirled and
played in the waves,
bringing in the new season.

They frolicked as
the tide washed out,
carrying the mermaids to
the dark depths of the sea.

In the morning, the cove looked the same as always.

But if you look very closely,

you will see the mermaids were there.